Fog

(Sunlight can’t penetrate the fog)

1

Beach shore headlines in the local news paper

Its that time of year folks when the sea fog rolls in and engulfs us for a day or two. This Feak fog hits us every year as you all know.

But if you are a holiday maker then this fog comes down on us every year, and remains for a day or so normally. But this year I have been told by the weather team that it may stay for longer, maybe three days.

This fog will be thick and will block out those sunny days folks so now is the time to prepare for the fog.

Please stay inside your homes or bed and breakfasts, and try not to walk the streets, and do nor drive your cars this can be very dangerous.

Business will be open well most of them this is up to the business owners. If you do need to go to the shops, be quick and don’t drive there.

Please only call the police if it is an emergency.

Brent Odell

Building up to the fog

2

Brent Odell opened up his cupboard in his small kitchen and smiled. The shelves were full of tinned food from tinned fruit to soups, and tinned meats and vegetables.

"Yes, sir I will be ready for this year's fog as always," he said to the empty kitchen.

Brent was single, and had been for a while now since his girlfriend had run off with a Spanish waiter while they had been on holiday. He had hated her for that, but now he looked back and thought what a let off.

She was bad news and his friends had never liked her, and now he could see why. Oh well we all make mistakes, and he smiled to himself.

She had done him a favour after all and now he could get on with his life, and besides he enjoyed being single. No one to tell him what to do he was now his own man.

He loved his job on the local newspaper, but the truth was a moron could write for the paper and the locals wouldn't know the difference. It was a local rag only, and the people who read it weren't that into it. They preferred the local gossip line that was also in existence by word of mouth.

Yes, the sad truth was that he was just a hack writer and he wrote what he liked most of the time, and the editor didn't give two hoots as long as the people bought the damned newspaper.

He read the latest headline on the front page, his headline about the fog and smiled. He wrote like shit and earned money what the hell is wrong with that.

Brent was a man of medium height and build he had never been into the gym scene. He was in his early thirties with short brown hair and a long nose. He was bullied at school because of his nose, being called beak face and big nose from the Monty python movie.

But he had a plan this fog year, he would go out and about talking to the locals and taking notes, and then when the fog cleared, he would write a big article on this year's long fog season.

"It's a great idea Brent," he said to himself and smiled again.

3

The stocky handsome man shouted out at the fat man in front of him, “Damn it Wayne can’t you move your fat arse,” the fat constable looked shocked, and saw that he was in the way and moved quickly.

The stocky man moved onto his office, and slammed the door shut.

“You done it now fat boy,” Donnell said a black man who was also short and stocky like his boss Cromwell.

“Yeah man you have pissed him off and now he will take it out on all of us,” whined Cliff an old boy at sixty-four and looking forward to retiring soon. He was plump, but not as plump as Wayne.

“Fuck you lot,” Wayne said looking at his buddies they always took the piss out of him. He didn’t mind really, and got on well with them.

"Stop whining like a little fat girl Wayne," the duty sergeant Damien said smiling at Wayne.

"Sorry sir but I'm always the butt of jokes in this place," Wayne whined.

Damien was also on the plump side in fact only the old boy Cliff was thin. This was beach shores police crew, and now was the busy times with fog season first, and then the holiday season after.

The office door opened and out stepped Cromwell he looked at his three constables, and then at the desk sergeant Damien.

He had a stern look on his face and he addressed them all.

"Okay as you all know the fog will be coming down on us shortly. You have all worked the fog season and you know what I am about to say, but I will say it anyway."

He paused and looked hard at them all.

“We will all be on twenty-four-hour duty, and we will stay at the station until the fog clears. There will be cots for us in the cells, and we will take it in turns to sleep.”

He looked at them all and added, “So any questions.”

They all knew the drill, and they all shock their heads. Cromwell was just about to turn back to his office.

“Oh, sir I got one question,” Wayne said smiling at the captain.

Cromwell gave him a hard look and replied, “Go on Wayne.”

“So, we will be eating take aways again like last year.”

The year before they had to bring in their own food, but last year they had lived on take aways for the day.

“God Wayne you and your bloody food,” Donnell said in disgust.

“Fuck you Donnell I only asked because this year the fog will stay longer,” Wayne said looking hurt.

“Leave him be Donnell,” Cliff put in.

“I will answer you Wayne, yes we will be eating take aways okay I have budgeted for that,” Desk sergeant Damien said.

“Good now we know where we stand okay,” Cromwell said and gave them one last look before going back into his office and closing the door this time.

“Man, what a silly question, are we going to get take aways,” Donnell said in a girlie voice.

Cliff and Damien laughed and Donnell smiled as did Wayne.

“You guys drive me mad,” Wayne laughed.

“Come on lads get your work faces on now,” Damien said and they all returned to their desks waiting for some action.

4

Oscar Holman smiled life was sweet at the moment even with this damned fog rolling ever closer. He was in his fifty's, and owned the local estate agents.

Business was normally slow in this town, but just lately things had picked up big time. All of his flats and houses for rent had gone, and even the big red barn that sat empty in a field had been swept up.

It seemed to him that this years longer than normal fog had attracted a lot in interest from outsiders, and they were going crazy snapping up all of his property's.

He looked across at Lilian and smiled. The office was small with two desks and a filing cabinet, and some pictures of houses on the walls.

"Business is looking up this year," he said to her looking at her big breast that were on show with her low-cut top.

"People have gone crazy," she replied laughing.

Oscar ran a hand through his short grey hair, and winked at her. Again, his eyes dropped to her large breasts, and she saw this and smiled. She wore far too much make up, but she was a damned good-looking woman.

Lilian like to tease men and she had to admit it turned her on when men looked at her breasts. She was in her thirties and married to Ray. They had no children yet, but it was early days they had only been married just over a year.

"If things keep on going like this, I will make a fortune," Oscar said looking at her breasts.

"Then you can take me out for a slap-up meal," she said smiling at him.

'God she was a fucking cock tease' he thought and felt his penis growing stiff in his boxer shorts. 'Better not get up until the fellow goes down a bit' he thought and smiled at her.

5

The duck and goose pub was a small place with a bar that ran along one wall. There was a dart board to one side, and tables and chairs in the middle with an old-style juke box in one corner.

The juke box had been brought by the owner because he wanted to make the place look like an American diner at one point, but it never worked. The truth was it looked more like the 'slaughtered lamb' from the horror movie 'American werewolf in London.'

Freddie sighed and carried on washing up glasses behind the bar. He had owned the bar for twenty years now, and still loved the place. There was no better smell than the smell of stale beer that's what he would tell people.

He was a big man with a large belly and a barrel chest and thick set arms. With his bald head and grey goatee beard he looked a real mean mother.

“Hi Freddie how are you,” said a voice and he looked up and smiled at his barmaid Rosemary.

She was young in her twenties and a good-looking lass with large breasts that the punters loved to ogle at. She was good at her job, and Freddie liked her.

“Hello love I’m fine, and how are you today,” he replied.

“Oh, I’m fine I was just wondering about the fog season,” she said to him coming round the bar to help him.

“I’ve decided to stay open during the fog and I hope that the hours will suit you love,” he smiled at her he was a big teddy bear really.

“So, what are the hours.”

“We will do the lunch time twelve until three, then the evening shift will be eight until twelve midnight.”

Last year Freddie had closed the pub, but got a lot of stick from customers who wanted a beer during fog time. So, he had decided to open this fog season.

“Those hours are fine Freddie.”

“Look Rosemary I’m not trying to be funny, but I have a spare room upstairs that you can use during the fog it will save you from walking in it.”

Freddie lived alone since his wife had died ten years ago, but he always kept a spare room, and he knew it was not safe to walk about half blind in the thick fog. He knew that Rosemary lived with her parents which was quite a way from the pub.

Rosemary looked at her boss and smiled she had been worried about walking in the fog.

“I will bring my stuff tomorrow thank you so much Freddie,” and then she hugged the big man.

“You are so welcome love,” he whispered in her ear.

He and his wife had never had children, but he knew in his heart that he would have made a wonderful dad. He was starting to think like Rosemary was the daughter he had never had.

"That's great it will be so good to have somebody in the old place again," he beamed at her.

She smiled at him she knew that he was lonely since his wife had died, and she guessed that she was really doing him a favour rather than the other way round.

But it benefitted them both.

6

Beans and burgers the sign read outside, and it was the place to meet for the youngsters of beach shore. Bernie the owner sold a wide choice of tasty burgers plus chilly beans, curry beans, sweet and sour beans, Mexican beans the list went on.

Bernie sighed it was quiet today, they had only a small number of customers. Bernie was in his forties with a large belly, and stubby arms and legs. He was short almost dwarf like, but not quite that small.

He lived close by and was a single man who enjoyed running his business, and that was all he had time for these days.

“Hey Leroy why don’t you give the kitchen a deep clean since we are not busy,” Bernie called over to his chef.

Leroy a large wide and tall black man smiled, and give Bernie the thumbs up, “Sure thing boss might as well stay busy.”

Leroy ran the kitchen on his own, with Bernie helping him from time to time when it got too busy.

Bernie saw his two waitresses chatting he didn’t blame them there was nothing to do.

“Hey girls what are you chatting about,” Bernie said walking over to them. The eating area had tables and chairs running down both sides, and pictures of the sea and countryside on the walls. The kitchen was separated from the eating area by a wooden door.

“Nothing much Bernie,” Sandy said giving him a wicked smile. She was single and slim, and nice looking, and a bit of a flirt with the men.

“Nothing much my back side,” Bernie said smiling at the two women.

“Nothing for a man to hear that’s for sure,” Sandy winked at him.

“Sandy pack it in you are such a tease sometimes really,” Lauren said. She was a bit older than Sandy, and was a single mum. But like Sandy she was also slim, and good looking.

“Oh, I don’t mind,” Bernie winked back.

“I bet you don’t,” Lauren laughed.

“So, Bernie we are staying open during the fog this year,” Sandy asked him. Last year they had stayed closed.

"Yes, this year we stay open the usual hours girls I hope you can both make it," he said looking from Sandy to Lauren, Leroy had already said no problem.

"Both girls nodded yes, "I will get a child minder that shouldn't be a problem," Lauren replied.

"Good girls I knew I could count on you, there will be a bonus in it for you as well."

"Great stuff," Sandy replied.

The usual hours were ten till one in the morning, then five till twelve at night.

7

The four bikes roared down the main high street of beach shore. Some of the old folk looking at the bikes in disgust "noisy bloody things," one old man said as they roared past him.

The young generation looked in awe at the big heavy looking bikes. "Cool," said one young boy wearing a baseball cap.

The leader of the biker gang known as the 'bust heads' always took the lead. 'Hulk' they never used their real names was a big bald man who enjoyed his food and beer far too much he was well over weight, and going on obese.

'Vamp' was a tall thin man and was almost skeleton like, and looked like a thin twig next to 'Hulk.' 'Vamp' was an evil bastard, and was waiting to take over as leader, and really cause some shit in this town.

'Wolf' was also a big man, but unlike Hulk he was a bear of a man with muscled arms which he like to show off with cut off tops. He liked 'hulk' and had no wish to take the lead.

Then there was 'Snake' he was the shortest in the gang and thin with it as well. He was a little bit two faced and would lie to get out of trouble that's why they called him 'snake,' he was also an evil son of a bitch.

Bringing up the rear was 'Panther' a huge black man with rippling muscles everywhere. He was heavily into body building, and no one messed with him. He was tall and wide like a brick shit house.

Later they sat drinking beer in their gang house, a large wooden shed in a field close to 'Hulks' house he owned the field.

"So, we going to fuck some people up when the fog hits," 'Snake' said with an evil grin on his skeleton face.

"Yeah man I like the sound of that," 'Vamp' put in, slapping hands with 'snake.'

"Maybe," Hulk replied rubbing his wobbly chin.

"Maybe we got the chance to fuck this town over," 'Snake' said in disgust.

“Damn right we have,” ‘Vamp’ said with a grin.

“I have to agree with snake for once ‘hulk’ this is a great chance to maybe rob and get some good stuff,” ‘Wolf’ said looking at the other gang members.

Panther nodded his head, and drank from his coke can he didn’t drink alcohol, “Yeah man wolf is right we get steal some good stuff, and maybe some money as well.”

“I’m not talking about stealing stuff I’m talking about fucking up some people, kicking in some heads,” ‘Snake’ said looking at ‘Hulk’ with a sneer.

“Right on brother,” ‘Vamp’ put in.

“Fuck off snake you evil little bastard and you vamp,” ‘Wolf’ almost shouted.

“Fuck you,” ‘Snake’ sneered at ‘wolf.’

“No fuck you snake you little fucking turd,” ‘Panther’ said getting to his feet.

Snake gulped and looked at the huge man in front of him, “Hey man no problem I will follow you guys anyway you know that,” ‘vamp’ sat with his eyes on the floor not looking at ‘Panther.’

‘Panther’ sat down and ‘Hulk’ got to his feet.

“We will cause some mayhem, and rob what we can, and if anyone gets in our way then maybe just maybe we will have a little fun with them okay,” he said looking from one to the next.

“Cool,” replied ‘snake’ he really hopped that someone would get in their way.

The others nodded yes, “Okay then tonight we get pissed, then tomorrow we own this town,” ‘Hulk’ said and they all cheered.

8

Ernie shepherd smiled at the little kids playing in the street by his sweet shop. But he wasn't smiling because he liked to watch them play, no he was smiling because he hoped a speeding car would plough into the little fuckers.

You see Ernie hated the kids, and he would watch the little fuckers in his shop like an eagle to see if they would steel from him.

He hoped they would and he would catch them, and then he would beat them before calling the police. Ernie was one mean old coot. He lived alone upstairs in the flat above the sweet shop, and was rarely ever seen going out.

He would stock up on food for the month so he wouldn't have to go out. He had never married, but had a few girlfriends in his younger days, he had been good looking then.

Now he was wrinkled and old with pure white hair cut short and a beard that was unkept. He had mean little green eyes, and watched his shop like a hawk.

He would stay open during the fog, and see if any of the little fuckers came in. They would think he would be easy in the fog, but he had his new best buddy Billy the baseball bat.

The day before the fog was due a row of cars and caravans, and small lorries came into the town of beach shore. Then once in the town they began to split up. Some parked outside bed and breakfasts, while others went into car parks with the caravans. A row of cars went to the big red barn in the field and parked outside.

The town prepared for the fog some businesses would close for the duration of the fog while a lot were staying open. Most people would stay indoors, but they were glad of the option of going out if they got too bored.

The town went to sleep that night tomorrow, would be a whole new day.

Andrew sighed and walked through the empty changing rooms. The swimming pool had closed for the day, and in fact had closed now until the fog lifted.

Andrew was glad the swimming baths would close it would give him more time on his games console. He loved playing games, and would spend the whole three days glued to his video monitor.

He clapped his hands all was clear no little brat playing hide and seek with him. The clap echoed around the empty changing room, and Andrew hurried out it had spooked him.

He checked the main hall, and then went into the swimming area. He would check the pump room and then close up, and go home and immerse himself in his games. He lived alone in a studio flat so no one would disturb him, and he had loads of pot noodles, and tins of soup and coke.

He smiled he was all set he checked the pump room all was good, and then he stood by the swimming pool, and looked at the cool water.

Then something entered his head a thought no not a thought a command.

'The water needs to be drained Andrew' the voice inside his head said.

"But I can't do that Mr Pearson will be well mad at me," Andrew said out loud.

'The pool needs to be drained Andrew now' the voice said inside his head.

“Yes, you are right I need to drain the pool,” Andrew walked to the pump room like a zombie. He pressed the switch to drain the pool. He went beside the swimming pool again, and watched as the water drained out.

‘Wait a little while and then I will tell you what must be done next’ the voice said.

Andrew sat on the small diving board, and waited he starred into space.

After a while the swimming pool was empty and Andrew stood by the end at the deep end. It was a long way down.

‘Okay Andrew now I want you to jump into the deep end’ the voice said.

Andrew tried to fight the voice inside his head, he didn’t want to die he wanted to play video games.

“I can’t do that and you can’t make me,” Andrew almost shouted out.

‘Jump into the deep and now’ the voice hissed inside his head.

Andrew closed his eyes, and tried to block out the voice but it was a losing battle the voice was so strong.

“No please,” Andrew called out.

‘Do it now Andrew’ the voice insisted.

Andrew walked into the air and then fell to the hard tiled floor below. He broke both legs, and the bones protruded from both legs. The voice released him, and he cried out in pain it was pure agony.

“Help me for the love of god please,” he shouted out, but the swimming baths were empty.

Fog day one

9

Glen whistled as he walked in the thick fog you couldn't even see the sun light it was that thick. His jack Russell Monty pulled on the lead, "Okay boy we are nearly there," Glen laughed.

Glen was in his sixty's and lived alone apart from his beloved dog Monty. He worked at the small local supermarket, but they only had a skeleton crew on during the fog so he told them he would rather stay home than work, which was fine by them.

Then Glen was treading in the sand they had reached the beach, and he let Monty off his lead. He heard the dog splashing in the sea water Monty loved the sea.

"Good boy Monty," Glen called out.

Glen looked around him the fog was so thick a person could creep up on you and you wouldn't even know it, he shuddered.

"Come on Monty time to go home boy," he called out.

Then Monty started to bark, and then the dog started to growl.

"Monty what is it boy I can't see you," Glen shouted out.

Then Monty yelped, and then went silent.

"Monty boy are you okay," Glen moved nearer to the water's edge, and felt his feet getting wet.

Then he turned, and almost bumped into a girl!

"I'm sorry," he stuttered and looked at her she must have been in her early twenties, and she was beautiful and naked. He couldn't help himself, and he looked at her small breasts with her pointed nipples, and then he went down further and saw the small mound of dark pubic hair.

"Like what you see grandpa," the girl giggled.

"What the hell," Glen turned and started to walk fast away from the girl. He was too old for all this shit.

Then Glen stopped and saw the tall thin man in front of him, right in front of him. The man wore all black with a long black coat, and a fedora hat.

"Go to her old man," the man said in a cold unemotional voice.

"I can't I need to find my dog I think," Glen stuttered out.

"Go to her now," the man's eyes flashed red, and Glen turned and walked back towards the naked girl.

"I'm so glad you came back to me grandpa," the girl giggled.

"Please help me find my dog," Glen said as he starred at the naked girl.

"Come here first grandpa," the girl said, and Glen walked right up to her.

She wrapped her arms around him and then opened her mouth wide to reveal two sharp fangs. She bit down into Glen s neck and began to drink hungrily.

Pete 'pee pee pants' walked as fast as his small legs would take him. He hated the fog it scared him, and he wished his mother hadn't forgotten the milk while shopping yesterday.

Now he had to hurry to the supermarket, and get a carton of milk. 'You are so much faster than mummy Pete be a darling it won't take you long,' she had pleaded with him, and of course he had gone.

He hated junior school and the children would taunt him every day with his nick name Pete 'pee pee pants.' He remembered that day his mother had told him to stand up to the bullies, then they would soon back down.

Good advice not.

That day he had stood up to the bully in front of everyone in the playground. But then he realised the bully was so much bigger than him, and the anger on the bully's face made Pete pee his pants.

"Look at him he has peed his pants," one of the girls had said laughing others started to point at his crutch and laugh. Then the bully had said "From now on you will be known as Pete pee pee pants."

Pete hurried through the thick fog and stopped he was losing his bearings. He looked back, and then looked forwards again or was he looking at the sides. He was lost.

He had been feeling the garden fences but when he had started to think back on that horrible day at school, he had somehow lost the feel of the fences.

"Pee pee pants," the voice said in the fog.

"Who is there is that someone from school," Pete said he was dead scared now.

"Are you going to pee your pants again," the voice laughed.

"Show yourself are you a coward," Pete said, but his voice was weak.

"Oh no I'm no coward pee pee pants," the voice laughed.

"So, who are you," Pete whined into the thick fog.

“I’m the devil,” a voice right next to him shouted into his ear!

Pete sobbed as he peed his pants again.

“Don’t worry Pete it will all be over so quickly.” The voice said and grabbed him from behind, he cried out as he was pulled into the thick fog.

Harry Russell or Mr Russell to everyone at the school was the principal of the local junior school. He was the only one in the school he had a lot of paper work to do, and would stay and finish it in the quiet.

He was a small round man with a bald head and glasses. But he could give the school kids a nasty stare if they were naughty.

He smiled his wife was waiting for him at home and she was making his favourite dinner tonight steak and kidney puddings.

He loved his wife Doris, but boy could she talk and that was why he decided to do his paper work in the school, he would never get it done at home.

He put his head down, and concentrated on his work then he heard a sound coming from the corridor outside his office.

He listened it was a kind of scrapping sound like someone running their finger nails down the wooden doors.

“Hello is anyone there,” he called out and added, “You had better go before I get up you shouldn’t be here.”

He looked out at the thick fog through his office window and shuddered it gave him the creeps, but there was no fog inside the school thank God.

He sighed and went back to his work, “Hey Baldy,” a voice called out and laughed.

He stood up and rushed over to the door and opened it, and looked outside one way and the other the corridor was empty.

“I’m warning you if a find you, you will be in big trouble,” he called out.

He walked into the corridor and then a class room door opened just down the way. He looked at the open door and felt butterflies in his stomach.

“Hey this is not funny at all,” he called out anger in his voice.

He slowly walked towards the open door and stopped, he took a deep breath and walked into the class room.

A young girl sat at a desk and she was looking at the large black board.

“Who are you,” he said he did not recognize her at all.

“I want to learn,” the girl said she had long blonde hair and was a pretty girl of about ten.

He was about to say something when another voice said “I want to learn to.”

He looked to his left a dark-haired girl sat at another desk looking at the black board.

“What is going on here,” he asked them.

Then he turned and looked at the black board, and gasped, the words ‘we want to learn how to kill you’ were written in bold.

The two girls stood up and now he could see their red eyes and sharp looking fangs. He turned and raced for the door only for there to be a tall thin man wearing all black in his way.

The man wore a fedora hat, and he starred hard at Harry, “Sit down Harry and let the girls take their medicine.”

Harry sat down at a desk, and the two girls took him one on each side.

Mike the motor mechanic sat down in his small work shed reading the local paper. He was open during the fog, but didn’t expect a lot of trade. He put the kettle on for a cup of tea. He looked round his work shop the shelf full of tyres and car parts the sunken pit so he could look at the underneath of the cars.

He was pleased with his life, and so enjoyed fixing cars he was a happy man. His wife and two kids were at home, and he would join them soon he was thinking of closing early.

Then he heard a car pull up outside. The fog was thick outside, but didn't enter the inside of the work shop. He went outside, and could make out a black BMW a real smart car.

The window rolled down, and he saw a black man inside. The black man was thin and had short curly hair, and a pleasant looking face.

"Hi their mate," Mike said to the black man.

"Hi can you look at my car I think I got a leak in the petrol tank," the black guy replied.

"Okay drive it onto the pit and I will take a look," Mike smiled.

"Okay can you guild me in," the black man asked.

Mike stood inside and the car slowly followed him. He walked onto the tracks over the pit, and waved his hands at the car looking at the tyres to make sure they were on the tracks.

There was a wall behind Mike now, and he called out, “Okay mate you can stop her there.”

The car suddenly shot forwards and hit Mike, and forced him back into the wall. His legs were crushed, and he cried out in pain.

“For fuck sake what did you do that for,” he cried out he was losing a lot of blood.

The black man got out of the car and walked around to him, “Don’t you die on me yet I need to feed,” then the black man opened his mouth to reveal two sharp fangs.

Mike cried out again as the man bit into his neck.

Doris Russell was making her husbands favourite dinner steak and kidney puddings. The potatoes and vegetables were on the boil, and everything was in order.

Then the front door bell went.

Who could that be Harry had his keys, and who would walk around in this thick fog?

Doris went to the front door and paused maybe Harry had forgotten his keys yes that must be it.

Doris opened the door, and saw two small boys.

“Sorry miss we are lost,” sobbed one of the boys he was wearing a blue coat the other boy wore a white coat. They looked like brothers and were very similar.

Doris looked out at the thick fog and shuddered anything could be hiding in that fog.

“What am I to do with you two then,” she said with her hands on her wide hips.

“Please we are scared of the fog miss,” this time it was the boy in the white coat who spoke.

"Oh well come inside you poor mites," Doris ushered them into the front room, and sat them down on the sofa. The living room had a large television on one wall, and a cabinet with plates and cups inside. Pictures of her and Harry were on the side board.

"Do you go to the local school my Harry is the head master there," Doris said proudly.

The boy in the blue coat shook his head, "No we never go to school."

"Oh, my that is so sad," Doris replied.

"Not sad its good," the boy in the white coat answered.

"What about your parents," Doris looked from one to the other the boys were so pale.

"Fuck them," Blue coat laughed.

Doris put her hand to her mouth, "Oh my such bad language."

"Fuck you cunt," white coat said and both boys opened their mouths to reveal their shining white fangs.

All Doris managed to say before they both attacked her was, "Oh my what big teeth you have."

10

The biker gang roared down the high street, they revved their bikes up loud, but they weren't going at a great speed even for them it was far to dangerous in the dense fog.

Hulk slowed his bike down even more there was a man on the pavement. As he drew close, he could see the man he knew him.

Hulk pulled over to the side just after the man.

"See that fucker behind us I know him," Hulk said as the bikers gathered round him.

"Yeah, I know that cunt as well," Vamp said a mean look in his eye.

"He walks like a faggot," Wolf said and laughed.

"Yeah, I bet he takes it up the arse," Snake sneered.

"So, what the fuck are we going to do," Panther asked.

"Watch this keep close to me," Hulk said and turned his bike around and slowly began to catch up with the man on the pavement.

As he got closer, he kicked out at the man hard, the man went flying into a brick wall hitting his head. Hulk laughed, and signalled the gang to follow him as he quickened up his speed a little.

"Was that it I would have killed the cunt," Snake hissed under his breath as he followed Hulk.

The man sat against the wall he could feel blood running down the side of his face, "Fuckers," he swore at the departing bikes.

He knew the bike gang and had a few run ins with them they were a bunch of cowards.

He could no longer hear the bike gang, and he began to rise, but felt giddy so he sat back down.

The fog was so thick he could barely see his legs. Then he saw a snake on his leg, "What the fuck," but no it wasn't a snake at all it was a hand and arm.

Then the hand gripped his leg hard, and he was pulled screaming into the fog.

The man and woman drove through the streets in the thick fog. The car was going at a snail's pace.

"Oh, Scott why did we have to come out in this I don't like it," the woman moaned besides him.

"Look Shona it's my mum I must get to her she is all alone," Scott sighed leaning forwards, and looking into the fog.

"I know that darling, but she will be fine she is a strong woman," but Shona knew it would do no good Scott wanted to be with his mum.

"I have to be with her," Scott whispered.

They had been engaged for a year now, but there was no sign of any wedding, and Shona was getting fed up of waiting. She loved the tall skinny man, but he was definitely a mummy's boy and that worried her.

"Look there is a man in the road," Shona said pointing.

Scott looked through the fog, "It could be a coat."

Scott stopped the car just in front of the shape in the road.

"Maybe I should take a quick look just to make sure," Scott said and smiled at Shona.

"Don't leave me," Shona cried out the fog scared her big time.

"I won't be a minute love," and with that Scott got out of the car leaving the driver's side door open.

As Scott went round to the front of the car, he saw that the shape had moved farther away. That was strange, but Scott walked into the fog, and soon the fog swallowed him up.

Shona sat there and looked as Scott disappeared into the thick fog.

"Oh, for fuck's sake hurry up Scott," she said into the empty car.

The she heard a cry in the fog it sounded like Scott, but she couldn't be sure. Did she have to go out into the fog she didn't want to do that.

Then she turned to the driver's side, and saw a man sitting there!

"Fuck you scared the shit out of me," she said seeing that it wasn't Scott at all.

"Who are you and what the fuck are you doing in our car," she said, but she was scared really scared.

"Hi there," the man grinned he was all in black with a fedora hat on his head.

Then the back window smashed and a figure moved quickly into the car, and grabbed Shona's head pulling it back.

"I like my meals to be easy," the man in the hat said and leaned over her showing his fangs. He moved towards her exposed throat, and Shona closed her eyes and let out a sob.

Hector walked in the fog and he wasn't scared at all. He was tall for his young age, and was a champion boxer. Winning the local title at a town close by there was no boxing gym in beach shore.

He was turning sixteen in a few days, and would be boxing the seniors, and that made him happy. He would win a senior title next. He lived with his parents in town, but they originally came from Mexico.

He was sometimes teased at school for being a Mexican, but he soon put a stop to that with his fists. Now the kids in the school showed him respect.

He was out for a walk he wasn't going to stop training just because of the fog. But it was silly to run so he would take a long walk instead.

“Hector,” a voice said in front of him and he stopped he didn’t recognize the voice at all it seemed cold and with no emotion.

“Who is that,” he called into the fog.

Then a voice behind him said, “Hector,” he turned round.

“Cut it out now or you will be sorry,” he shouted into the fog.

“Hector,” behind him again and he turned round.

“Hector,” from the side of him.

“Hector,” from the other side.

“Cut it out now,” he screamed into the fog even he was getting scared now.

“Hector, Hector, Hector, Hector,” came the voice again and again, the voice was all around him now.

Then a figure was in front of him it was a woman, and she was very pretty with bright red lip stick.

"Behind you," the woman laughed, and then Hector was pulled backwards screaming into the fog.

Cromwell sighed it was so damned boring manning the police station. All his constables were out patrolling the streets not that many people would venture out in this thick fog. But then again maybe they would you could never tell with folks.

Then the switchboard flashed, and he was so stunned that he just looked at it for a few seconds then he picked it up.

"Beach shore police station how can I help you," he spoke clearly and loudly into the phone.

"I see okay I will get someone down there straight away you just hold on okay," then he turned off the caller, and picked up his radio.

"Wayne, Donnell you there over," he said loudly into the radio. He decided that Wayne and Donnell were better than the older pair Cliff and Damien.

It was Wayne who answered, “Yes sir receiving you loud and clear.”

“There is an incident in Clyde Street get your butts over there now.”

“Okay boss we are on the way over,” the voice replied.

“Good now move it over and out,” Cromwell said and put down the radio.

Silly fuckers he thought there had been a car crash in Clyde Street who would drive around in this if not a policeman. Serves them right he thought.

“Hey fatty this is Clyde Street,” Donnell said pointing at a sign Wayne was just about to turn into Evans Street.

“Oh yes and stop calling me fat,” Wayne whined.

“Just go slowly fat face, and we should see something,” Donnell said smiling.

“You shouldn’t keep saying that to me its not right,” Wayne whined again, and added “You even made me pick up the radio, and I’m driving.”

Donnell laughed, “Give you some exercise fat boy.”

“Your so bad,” Wayne whined.

“Stop look a car in the middle of the road that must be it,” Donnell said and Wayne stopped the car.

“You go out and take a look I will wait here,” Donnell said.

“Why me your bigger than me,” Wayne said looking at his black partner.

“Look you go take a look and signal me okay,” Donnell smiled at Wayne.

Wayne sighed, and moved his bulky body out of the car.

Donnell watched as Wayne got closer to the car, and then he was lost in the fog.

Wayne moved closer and then went round to the back of the car all seemed to be okay. He shone his torch into the car it was empty. The car seemed to be in good condition.

“I like my men big,” he turned, and almost dropped his torch.

The woman was leaning against the car and she was stunning. Long red hair and a slim body with big breasts showing through her small top.

“What the fuck,” Wayne said.

“I want a fuck yes big boy,” the woman smiled at him.

Wayne got himself together and couldn’t believe his luck. He looked around there was only Donnell in the car not far away.

“Maybe we should go somewhere quieter,” Wayne grinned at the beautiful woman.

“I want it here big boy,” and she leaned back on the bonnet her small skirt lifting up.

“Holy shit,” Wayne moved towards her he was getting a hard on.

The woman wrapped her arms around him, and then he was kissing her his tongue moving inside her mouth. The pain exploded in his mouth as the woman ripped out his tongue with her teeth!

She moved her head away, and spat out the tongue Wayne stood there in shock. The woman grabbed him, and pulled his bloody mouth onto hers.

Donnell shifted in his seat damn that fat wanker Wayne was taking his time.

Donnell felt the car rock as something jumped onto the roof.

“What the fuck,” Donnell said looking upwards.

He got out of the car shining his torch, but he could not see anything on the car roof. He turned round and looked at the other car, and then something jumped onto his back!

He screamed as he felt pain in the side of his neck the thing held him in a vice like grip. He could feel the blood running out of his body as the thing that had attached itself to him fed.

Tim leaned over the lap top in his office he was doing staff appraisals. He was the manager of the beach shore supermarket, and he enjoyed his job. He had moved from London into the countryside beach town. He was single and nearing his fifties, but he didn't care he was enjoying himself that was all that mattered.

He sighed he had five staff working this shift Raymond the security officer, Tina working the counters, Paul filling the shelfs, and Ann and Tracy on the check outs.

Damn it he wished he had closed the store now it was so quiet hardly no one had decided to venture out in the fog.

Then he heard noises people talking, good that must be customers.

Tim switched off his lap top and then the light went out, he sat there in the darkness.

He could see light coming from under the door it had not been a power cut after all. Then his blood ran cold so who had switched off his office light!

“Who’s there I am calling the police,” he reached for the phone but it was not there. The phone was always there on his desk, but now it was missing.

He pulled out his mobile phone, and switched on the torch. He swung it round the room. The pictures on the walls the filing cabinet, and the man!

The man stood over by the filing cabinet he had bright green hair, and looked like a punk rocker.

“I’m going to make you suffer human,” the man said and then Tim was thrown across the room. He hit the wall hard, and slumped to the floor. He was picked up again and hurled across the room at the other wall.

He sobbed on the ground, “Please no more what do you want,” he sobbed again, “Is it money.”

Then the thing was right by his face, and he could smell its putrid breath, “I want your blood fucker.”

Raymond was watching the young girl closely he was sure that she was stealing. The group of people had wandered into the supermarket, and they were not locals he didn’t know any of them, and that bugged him.

The girl was wearing a summer dress with flowers all over it and she had long dark hair she must have been in her early teens.

Raymond saw her put two chocolate bars into her dress pocket.

“Got you bitch,” he whispered and smiled.

He loved it when he caught them stealing. The look of shock on their faces always cracked him up.

Raymond looked at the floor, and then down the aisle the girl had gone.

“Are you following me,” the voice said from behind him, and he turned and saw the girl. ‘How did she do that’ he thought, anyway it didn’t matter he had her now.

“I think you are stealing young lady,” he gave her one of his hard stares. Even though he was in his seventies he was still an active man, and could look after himself.

“What makes you think that,” the girl said in a cold voice.

“Come into my office and you can empty your pockets there,” he pointed to a closed door. The girl shrugged, and followed him.

Once inside the small room he said to her, "Okay now empty your pockets for me."

The room was small and the two only just managed to fit in any more and it would not have worked. There were rows of files on shelves, and that was it. But Raymond liked to bring them in here for privacy.

"Okay mister," the girl said and put her hand into her pocket, "What have I got here mister."

Raymond leaned forward, "Show me now."

The girl was quick and the knife came out in a flash, and cut right across Raymond's throat.

He stood there in shock, and then tried to stem the pumping blood with his hands. The girl moved his hands away, and started to fed on his throat. Letting the blood cover her summer dress.

Tina heard the voices, and smiled at last some customers. She saw Raymond walking down the aisle always looking for robbers.

Tina was working the counters the fish and meat counter the deli counter was closed. The fish and meat only had a limited stock on show. The store should have closed really.

Two men came up to the counter they were scruffy and wore old worn clothes. They looked like beggars.

"What shall we have mate," the taller of the two said looking at the meat counter.

"Buy the whole lot," the short man replied.

The taller man put a penny on the counter, "That should cover it," he winked at Tina. Tina wished she was at home with her two kids now, she didn't need this crap.

"Look if this is some kind of joke I will call security," Tina tried to sound pissed off, but her voice was shaky she didn't like the look of these two men.

"One penny and all the stock is ours that's the way it works lady," the short man said smiling, he had dirt on his face.

Tina couldn't see Raymond 'where the fuck was, he when you needed him, she thought.'

"Or maybe we can get something else," the taller man rubbed his crutch. Tina looked at him in horror.

"Yeah, she is a bit plump, but still worth a good shag," shorter man replied with a laugh.

The counters were quite high, but the men jumped over them as if they were nothing, and stood next to Tina!

"I," she moaned and then the men pulled her to the floor. Taller man attacked her throat, and the shorter man went for the wrist both drank thirstily.

"Hey boy do you like to hang around," the voice said and Paul turned round, and saw a man roughly the same age as him. But his clothes were scruffy, and torn in places.

“What do you mean by that,” Paul said he was filing the pet aisle.

“My two young sisters like people who hang around,” the man said.

Then Paul saw two little girls in tattered shorts and t-shirts.

They giggled at him, “They are both so hungry and haven’t eaten in a while now,” the man said.

“Oh, sorry to hear that maybe you can shop, and buy some food for them,” Paul said putting down the box of cat food.

Then Paul was punched in the face and he went down on his backside rubbing his jaw, “What the fuck did you do that for.”

“You will see my friend,” the man said and then he threw a rope over some pipes above on the supermarket ceiling. He tied the rope into a hoop at one end. The two girls continued to giggle.

Paul was going to get to his feet, but the man pushed him down with his boot. Then the hoop was put on Pauls legs and the man pulled it tight.

“Hey that hurts man,” Paul cried out maybe Raymond would hear him, and come to his aid.

Paul was lifted up into the air by his feet as the man pulled the other end of the rope. Then he tied it around a piece of metal shelving. Paul swung and looked at the man in front of him upside down.

“Now we feed my sisters,” the man said, and the two girls giggled.

The man cut Paul’s throat open and then pushed him so that he swung from side to side. The man and the two girls were on their knees under the swinging Paul, and the blood poured down onto their faces and clothes, and the three drank hungrily.

“I can hear peoples voices,” Tracy said smiling.

“Good maybe we can do some work now, Ann replied to her friend. They had both worked part time at the supermarket since having their first babies. They spent a lot of time together, and people thought that they were sisters.

Ann lived with Martin and Tracy was a single mum her boyfriend having left as soon as he heard about her being pregnant.

Tracy had the big breasts that men were always looking at while Ann was slim and fit looking.

One minute the tills were empty, and the next they were full of people! Tracy looked at Ann as if to say how did that happen. Two women stood by Tracy they wore tattered clothes, and they smelt bad behind them were five men all tattered as well.

Ann had a woman with a baby in her arms, behind her were about six or seven people all in rags.

"My god where did you all come from," Ann said in shock.

"I like her big tits," a small boy said, and Tracy looked down at the dirty face of a boy.

"Do you mind," Tracy said firmly.

"We want to buy the whole store," a man said he had wild brown hair.

"Yes, the whole fucking place," another man shouted he had short dirty blonde hair.

"Well, you can't buy the whole place," Ann said she was scared, but didn't want to show it.

"Hey cut that out," Tracy shouted as one man grabbed her large breasts.

"You there is no need for that," Ann shouted out.

Then a man appeared behind Ann and started to rub both of her small breasts, "Hey fuck off," Ann said, and tried to get his hands off, but he was strong.

"Leave her alone you brute," Tracy said, but then she felt hands all over her breasts as two men worked on them.

"Fuck this shit," a man with bright green hair said and added, "Take them now."

Tracy and Ann were pulled away from the checkouts and stripped of their clothes then the group of people began to fed on their throat's arms legs any space available to them.

Day two

11

The man in all black with the long coat, and fedora hat took centre stage. The make shift stage had been erected at the end of the big barn that was rented.

“Abraham, we love you,” came a cry from the audience.

“Thank you, my brethren you are, all here I take it,” Abraham looked out, and saw the nodding heads.

“You all had fun yesterday I take it,” Abraham smiled as the crowd roared and cheered.

“We haven’t had so much fun in years master,” came a shout.

“Good I’m only sorry I never found out about this fog years ago, but we travel so much, and hardly ever hear the news or read the newspapers.”

Abraham looked out and saw that no one was bothered about that they would follow him until the end of time.

Then the green haired punk rocker stepped up, “Abraham we need to make sure that the brethren put their kills into the swimming pool.”

Abraham smiled at his second in command, “Yes Benedict you are right please when you kill put the bodies into the swimming pool.”

“I put went to put mine in the other day and saw some human in pain at the bottom,” a man said with his arm raised.

“Ah that would be Andrew, I made him jump and brake both of his legs badly,” Abraham said with a grin on his handsome face. Unlike the others he was always clean.

“I hope you threw your body on top of him,” Benedict asked the man.

The man nodded yes, “Good we have to make these humans suffer as much as possible,” Benedict added.

“So anyway, my brethren,” Abraham looked at his wrist watch, “Today is another day now so go out and feed, and have some fun.”

The bikers roared down the road that was next to the beach the sea breeze rolling in. Hulk stopped and the others followed he could smell the sea it was a good smell.

Hulk looked into the dense fog anything could be lurking inside hiding and waiting for someone to come in.

But he wasn't scared he had to show them that he was the boss.

He revved his bike and shot forwards, and shouted out "A race you fuckers to the stop sign up ahead."

Snake gunned his bike and cursed, "You fucking cheat."

They all knew there was a stop sign at the end of the beach road.

Hulk went into the fog and laughed he enjoyed winding them up especially Snake he was one to watch.

Hulk reached the stop sign and turned his bike around, and waited for the others. He couldn't wait to see Snakes face the little creep. He heard screams and shouting in the fog, and then silence. Then four bikes rolled out of the fog minus there riders.

Hulk starred in horror as the bikes came to a stop and fell over. He gunned his bike, and took a slip road, and raced away terror in his heart.

Vamp couldn't see anything as he raced towards the stop sign, he wanted to beat Hulk. He should be boss not that fat fucker Hulk. He wasn't going that fast to dangerous, and then he heard a voice from above him, "Charlie you wanker,"

That was his real name no one called him by his real name he stopped the bike. "Who is that you had better show yourself fucker."

Vamp took out his blade, and looked upwards. A shape came darting down, and he screamed as he was plucked off the bike and carried upwards.

Panther slowed down and Wolf also slowed down they were close together.

"Did you hear that scream," Panther asked Wolf.

"Yeah man it was close as well," Wolf replied.

The two men looked comical on their bikes they were so big. Wolf was like a bear, and Panther had muscles on his muscles.

"Charlton you black fucker you look like a faggot," a voice in the fog said laughing.

Panther looked at Wolf in wonder, "Who the fuck was that," Panther asked.

Wolf shrugged his big shoulders, "David I hear that you take it up the arse," another voice said laughing.

"What the fuck, and they know our real names the motherfuckers," Wolf spat out.

"You are going to pay you cunts," Panther shouted into the fog.

Then shapes started to walk from the fog, and the two men saw that they were surrounded. The shapes were of men and women, and even a few kids as they got closer the two men could smell the smell of death.

“I don’t think so,” said a small boy and laughed, and then the circle of people jumped onto the two bikers as one.

Snake heard the scream, and slowed down that sounded like Vamp, but he couldn’t be sure. Vamp was his rival he knew that Vamp wanted the leader job just as much as Snake did.

Hulk had out lived his leadership now, and it was time for one of them to take over, and Snake would be the one.

He would boss those two big motherfuckers around, that panther thought he was the bee’s knees because of all his muscles, well Snake would show him.

That wolf walked around looking like a bear with his big shoulders, and big belly.

“Richard, I hear you like little boys,” a voice called out from the fog.

Snake was stunned what the fuck, “Who is that,” he said into the fog.

“It’s the little boy you shagged up the arse,” the voice called back.

“I have never shagged a man or a boy you motherfucker,” Snake said, but he was scared.

“But I bet you would like to,” the voice said.

“Show yourself now, and I will cut you so bad fucker,” Snake took out his blade.

“Richard you are such a sad little runt,” the voice laughed hard.

“Stop calling me Richard I’m Snake,” he shouted out.

“Richard, Richard, Richard is a gay boy,” the voice mocked him.

Snake put the bike on its stand, and stood their blade in hand, “Come to me motherfucker.”

The shape was fuzzy in the fog, and then it came up close and Snake saw that it had green hair and was wearing punk rocker gear.

"So, fight me Richard gay boy," the green haired man laughed.

Snake lunged at the man, but he went forwards into thin air, and then was grabbed from behind. One arm around his throat the other on his arm that held the blade.

The man twisted his arm and Snake heard a crack as his arm broke, he screamed, and let go of the blade.

Then he smelt the smell of the dead on his face, and a sharp nail ran across his throat, "Time to die Richard," the man whispered into his ear.

Benedict rounded up his crew it had been fun killing and feeding on the biker gang, but there was still one left.

“Let’s give him a real scare,” Benedict said, and the others nodded and laughed.

“Okay start up the bikes, and roll them out of the fog he will be so scared when he sees that his buddies are no longer on them,” Benedict laughed.

Benedict heard the last biker roar away down a slip road, “No matter we will catch up with him later.”

Cromwell had left Cliff and Damien at the station to man the place he needed to get out. So, he patrolled the streets of beech shore. He slowly drove down the roads looking at shops, and seeing if any people were about.

He saw some dogs, and a cat but he saw no one, but then they could be hidden by the dense fog. The fog seemed to be worse this year thicker and more ominous, and it was lasting longer than previous years.

Maybe this was to do with global warming.

Then he saw a figure in the fog he couldn't make out who it was. He slowed the car down even more, and opened his window.

"Hey who is that," he called out loudly.

The figure stopped and saw the car and came up to the window it was Shirley West.

"Shirley what are you doing out in the fog," Cromwell asked the old lady. She lived on her own, and was well into her eighties, but she was always out and about.

"Hello Hudson how are you haven't seen you in ages my dear," the old woman gave him a big smile. No one called him by his first name these days it was always Cromwell, and he found that he wasn't used to it. But he would say nothing.

"Look Shirley its not safe to be walking in this fog please go home, I can give you a lift."

"Nonsense Hudson I can walk its only up the road, but thank you," she smiled at him again.

He looked at her wrinkled old face and white hair and smiled, “Okay Shirley you go home now.”

He watched her fade into the fog.

There was an alley way opposite from where he had stopped, and he looked into this. He could see nothing in the fog, and was about to put up his window when a voice came out of the fog.

“Hey copper down here.”

“Who is that show yourself,” Cromwell called into the fog.

“Come and get me copper,” the voice was cold sounding.

Cromwell got out of the car and took out his baton, and held it tight. He walked a little way into the alley. The fog was so thick he couldn’t see anything in front of him.

He had a bad feeling about this, and then a voice from beside him said, “Copper I’m here.”

He turned then from the other side, “No I’m here copper.”

Then there was a crash of metal as he heard a car crash close by. Cromwell took one last look around, and then ran back to the patrol car.

“Later Copper,” the voice laughed behind him.

“Send a car to Argyle Street officer injured,” the voice on the other end of the line said.

Cliff asked, “Can you give me more details, and who is this speaking please.”

The line went dead.

“Shit one of our unit is injured in Argyle Street Damien,” Cliff said turning to his buddy.

“I will go,” Damien said he was the desk sergeant but was getting bored inside the station.

Cliff didn't mind at all he didn't want to go out into the fog alone, "Okay Damien that's fine I will man the station."

"Good man I won't be long could be a hoax caller."

"Could be mate see you soon," Cliff saw his buddy move out of the station.

"Now time for a coffee," he said and walked into the small kitchen. He was looking forward to retiring soon, this year the fog really unnerved him for some reason.

Damien reached Argyle Street and cruised down the road he saw nothing. He cruised down the street again, nothing it must have been a hoax caller after all.

Then a figure came into view right in front of his car he slammed on the brakes, not that he was going fast, but he still could have injured her.

The woman slapped her hands on the bonnet, and glared at him. He shuddered there was something not right about her.

“You could have killed me copper,” she spat out.

He opened his door and climbed out, and went up to the woman. She was small and plump with dark hair and a very pale plain looking face.

“I’m sorry miss can you please go home,” he didn’t know her maybe she was a tourist, they liked to come when the fog was around.

“I don’t live here moron,” she spat.

“Hey there is no need for language like that miss.”

“I’m not a miss I’m a whore, and I like to suck big cocks,” she laughed at him.

“Now that’s enough go or I will arrest you,” he tried to sound angry, but it didn’t work he was scared all of a sudden.

"Arrest me you creep you just try it," she stood there with her hands on her hips.

"Please just move on."

"Arrest me fucker."

"Now that's enough okay I'm warning you."

"Fuck off cunt," she spat at him.

He moved towards her, and then saw more figures coming out of the fog. Like her they wore tattered clothes, and were dirty looking.

"Arrest all of us copper," the woman laughed, and the crowd of people closed in around him.

"Hey wait now please you can't do this," he pleaded with them. Then they grabbed him, and he screamed as hungry feeding noises came out of the fog.

Cromwell stopped his patrol car, and saw the wreak in front of him. He got out and walked over to the smashed-up police cruiser. It was Donnell and Wayne's without a doubt.

It looked like someone had smashed it up with a sledge hammer, and they had made a damned good job the car was a mess. Glass littered the road, and metal was beaten inwards.

“Holy shit what the hell happened here,” he said to himself.

He shone his torch inside the wreak, but there was no body inside, and then he made a quick check on the outside.

Nothing.

He looked into the fog and shivered, something bad was going on in his town. He hurried back to his car.

Hulk stood inside the furniture shop he had just broken in, and the alarm was sounding, but he didn’t care. Tears of frustration and hurt ran down his fat face. He had lost his whole gang in a matter of minutes.

There was something inside the fog and it scared him badly, and it made him angry at the same time.

He looked around at the chairs and tables the nice big sofas, and the side boards, and classy mirrors on the walls. He needed to let out his frustration.

He saw the fire axe, and moved over to the glass case. He saw a bulky looking ash tray on one table and picked it up it was heavy. He smashed the glass and took out the axe.

"This is for you guys," he roared.

He began to smash up the tables, and then he smashed every single mirror on the walls, and then he started on the nice-looking sofas.

He was a mad man, and he didn't stop until he was utterly exhausted.

Brent Odell walked through the thick fog, he was looking forward to going back home soon, and warming up some tinned vegetable soup.

He had seen a few people out and about he had even seen a police cruise not long ago. He held his latest gadget in his hand a spy glass. It was black and small, and fitted nicely into his hand. He could look through it and zoom right in it would come in handy in this damned fog.

He stopped just in front of him was the out line of a man he was smoking, and leaning against a fence. He couldn't make out who it was. Then a woman appeared, and Brent put the spy glass up to his eye.

He saw that the woman was attractive long blonde hair and a pale pretty face. But her clothes were shite, she was wearing rags.

"This spy glass is so cool," he whispered to himself.

He still couldn't see the man, but he must have been a local. Then the two were kissing and as Brent watched the man suddenly went stiff, and he saw blood on the man's neck.

The woman was biting the man's neck and drawing a thin line of blood. Then the woman looked his way, and he saw her blood shot red eyes, and she was sucking the blood from the man's body. She seemed to smile at Brent, and he nearly pissed himself.

Brent dropped his hand, and ran into the fog. His mind was going at a hundred miles an hour the woman had been a vampire. He had never believed in vampires, but he had just seen it with his own eyes.

Brent ran home and didn't stop until he was inside his front door. He locked the door and stood there panting. So much for a book about the three days of fog he would write one about real vampires.

Cliff was getting spooked the police station was so scary when no one was about. He kept hearing creaking and other noises, but he knew it was just the building settling.

“I’m too old for this now,” he said out loud he was looking forward to retiring next year with a nice police pension to boot.

He heard a creak, and looked that way nothing of course. He hopped Wayne was okay he liked Wayne, and felt sorry for the way the others talked to him.

He needed to pee badly, and headed towards the toilet. He heard another creak it was just the old wooden floor boards.

He tutted and smiled to himself, ‘what an old fool.’

He went into a cubicle and locked the door, and stood there and peed. “Aaahh that’s better,” he said out loud.

“Cliff,” the voice said it was just above a whisper.

“Who’s there,” Cliff demanded.

“Cliff,” this time the voice was louder.

“Look I’m a police officer,” he called out, but he didn’t open the cubicle door.

“Cliff you old fart,” then laughter.

Cliff was scared he had never felt so scared in all his years.

The voice didn’t sound normal at all, it sounded like a sound from a dead man’s throat.

“Please go away,” Cliff said now he sounded scared as well.

“It’s okay Cliff, I won’t make you suffer,” the voice said.

Then added, “For too long.”

The cubicle door was kicked inwards and it struck Cliff on the shoulder, and sent him backwards onto the toilet. He sat there and looked up at the man wearing all black with a hat on his head.

“Time to die old man,” then Cliff screamed as the man reached for him.

Cromwell drove through the streets of beach shore, why would someone smash up a police cruiser, and more important where were his constables.

Even with his head lights on full beam it was hard to see so he had to go slow. Luckily, he knew the town like the back of his hand.

Then he stopped the car and gasped!

He starred at the scene in his head lights.

A dying man was in the middle of the road, and there were four things feeding on him. Because that's what they were doing feeding on him. The poor man moved now and again, but he must have been weak.

Cromwell saw two things hungrily sucking up blood from the man's wrists. One was at his bloody throat while the fourth was biting into his leg. The trousers having been ripped off the man.

Then the thing on the man's throat suddenly looked at Cromwell, and smiled blood covered his face. Then the other three looked at him.

Cromwell could not believe his eyes they were vampires, and they wore tatty clothes, and were dirty like they had just come from the grave. Vampires surely not, but they were right there in front of him.

“Holy god,” Cromwell said and put the car into gear, and raced away from the bloody scene his heart racing like a steam train. He didn’t care about speed he wanted to be away from the street.

Cromwell banged on the church door. The two massive wooden doors looked strong, and could hold back a crowd. One door was opened, and a small priest looked at Cromwell, and ushered him inside.

Father Michael was a small plump old man with receding hair and glasses on his long nose. He was a kind and gentle man, and worked wonders for the town. Everyone liked Father Michael.

"Cromwell what's wrong you look terrible," Father Michael said with concern in his voice.

"Father you are not going to believe me, but you know me father, and you know I don't take shit from anyone," Cromwell looked at Father Michael.

"Tell me Cromwell."

"Look the fog is being used as a shade from the sun I have just worked that out."

"A shade from the sun what do you mean by that."

"Things are using the fog as cover against the sun light."

"Things."

"Yes, father things that have come to beach shore to feed on us."

"What things Cromwell."

Cromwell looked father Michael in the eye and said, “Vampires.”

Father Michael sat next to Cromwell on the pew, and didn’t say anything for a good few seconds.

“Okay Cromwell I know you are not a man to make wild things up,” he rubbed at his jaw line.

“You have to believe me father there are vampires out there, and they are killing the towns folk I’ve seen it with my own eyes, and my constables have gone missing.”

Cromwell sighed, and looked at the floor this was a nightmare.

Father Michael lay his hand on Cromwell’s shoulder, “I believe you, my son.”

Cromwell smiled, “I need to get as many people to this church, we will be safe here.”

Father Michael nodded, “Yes bring them here Cromwell and be swift for if what you say is true then surely, we don't have much time before the fog lifts."

"Very true father if we can save life's that will be a big bonus at least."

Cromwell got to his feet he was now on a mission to save as many people as he could.

Father Michael was at the altar now, "Before you go take these."

Cromwell slowly walked up to the alter, and saw that father Michael held a large golden cross.

"I can't take that it must be worth a fortune."

"Money is nothing compared to saving life's my son."

Cromwell took the cross, and Father Michael handed him two bottles of holy water.

"Thank you, father."

"May god bless you my son," and Father Michael made the sign of the cross over Cromwell.

12

Oscar Holman looked over at Lilian, and saw her big breasts almost spilling out of her low-cut top. Damn she was making him so horny.

“Pretty boring today,” he said to her.

She looked up from her magazine, “Well it was your idea to open during the fog.”

She was right, but the reason he wanted to open was to have her not get any custom.

He got up and walked over to her desk and pretended to look at her magazine, but his eyes were firmly on her breasts.

She smiled at him, “What are you looking at may I ask.”

God she was such a cock tease, “You know damn well what I’m looking at you are a fine-looking woman, Lilian.”

There it was out in the open now.

“But what about my husband Ray,” she said with a wicked smile on her lips.

“He will never know,” Oscar was going bright red in the face he was so worked up.

Lilian looked at the erection in his trousers, “Oh my you do look like a big boy.”

“God, I want you so bloody badly,” Oscar pulled down his zipper, and took out his erect penis.

“Oh, my you are big,” then Lilian had him in her mouth.

“Oh god that is so good,” Oscar closed his eyes.

Ray was in the garden feeding the hens, he enjoyed his hens they were interesting birds, and they were good layers. ‘We will never have to buy an egg again,’ he had said to his wife Lilian.

The fog was so thick in the garden he could hardly see anything. He loved his wife Lilian, but it bothered him her working for that bastard Oscar Holman. He was sure that the old fucker was after his wife.

“Raymond,” the voice came out of the fog.

"Who the fuck is that," Ray said into the thick fog. He was a tall man with board shoulders, and could handle himself in a fight.

Raymond listen to what I have to say," the voice came at him again.

Ray calmed down, "Okay tell me."

"Your wife is sucking Oscar Holman's cock right now as we speak."

"What the fuck," Ray replied.

"Now he is going to put his cock up her and fuck her hard you had better sort this out Raymond," the voice chuckled.

"My god who are you."

"Just believe what I say you can go and catch them at it."

"I got my rifle," Ray said he owned a rifle for hunting weekends with his mates.

"That's it Raymond get the rifle and sort this mess out now."

Ray hurried into the house.

Oscar entered Lilian from behind she was leaning over her desk. He fucked her hard, and sweat poured down his red face.

"Oh god this is so good," he shouted out pumping away inside her.

"Fuck me big boy, fuck me harder," she screamed at him.

Ray looked at them through the class door, they were going at it hammer and tong.

"The voice was right that fucking bitch," Ray said and opened the door.

Oscar shot his load as the little bell above the door went.

"Oh god I've come," he said, and looked over at the door.

Ray stood there with a rifle in his hands!

"Oh shit," Oscar pulled up his pants and trousers.

“Ray oh my god its not what it seems he forced me,” Lilian said pointing at Oscar, and pulled up her tint panties.

“Well, well, well I got a bitch and a cunt,” Ray said aiming the gun at Lilian then Oscar.

Please Ray no,” Oscar said putting his hands up.

“Shut up you cunt,” Ray hissed at him.

“Ray, he raped me you got to believe me,” Lilian said sitting on the edge of the desk.

“A rapist,” Ray looked at Oscar hard.

“She is lying I would never rape anyone,” Oscar’s face was bright red.

“So, your lying,” Ray turned to Lilian.

“No, I’m telling you the truth my darling please,” she whined at him.

Ray put the barrel of the gun close to Oscar’s face, “Suck it cunt.”

“What,” Oscar said looking at the barrel.

“I said suck the barrel you cunt.”

Oscar held the barrel, and then put it in his mouth, and closed his eyes.

“Good,” then Ray pulled the trigger, and Oscars brains hit the wall behind him.

Lilian screamed, and held her hands to her face.

“Now its your turn bitch,” Ray shot her twice in the chest. She slumped onto the floor dead.

Ray turned the rifle on himself, and shot himself in the head.

The door opened, and in rushed two men in tattered clothes.

“Shit, he has killed himself,” the shorter one said.

“Damn it we have missed out on a meal,” the other said.

“Never mind plenty of fish in the sea come on,” the short one said, and they both left the shop.

The duck and goose pub was quiet, but maybe it would pick up a bit later. Freddie sighed, and looked at the two old men drinking their beers and chatting.

Rosemary was cleaning the top of the bar, and looking for things to keep herself busy.

The door suddenly opened, and in rushed Cromwell!

"Look people we have got to get to the church it will be safe there," Cromwell said panting.

"Safe from what chief," Freddie asked looking at Rosemary and shrugging his large shoulders.

"There is something in the fog, and it is killing people please believe me," Cromwell looked at them all.

"What is in the fog chief," Freddie asked.

"Okay I will say it once and you must believe me," he paused and said the word, "Vampires."

"Vampires fuck me Colin that's a new one," the old man drinking his pint said to his mate laughing.

"Vampires my arse Tony," his mate replied sipping his pint.

"Look as soon as you see or hear anything then you will know its true, then you head for the church okay," then Cromwell turned on his heels and was gone.

"Wow do you think he is telling the truth," Rosemary said to Freddie.

Freddie shrugged, "I've known Cromwell a long time and he is not the sort to make up stories."

"Bullshit," Tony said from their table.

"God damn vampires he is on drugs mate," Colin put in.

"I suggest like the man said we keep our eyes and ears open," Freddie said to them all.

The two old men drinking just mumbled.

“I’m going down to the cellar to change that beer,” Freddie said smiling at Rosemary.

“Okay Freddie.”

The cellar was damp, and there were puddles of water on the floor. The cellar was small, and had windows at the top. One of the windows was open, and the cool air came into the cellar.

“Damn it the rain will get in,” Freddie said and reached up and closed the window.

The lights went out, and Freddie stood in total darkness.

“Shit, he reached for the light switch, but nothing happened. He was always saying he would put a torch down in the cellar now he wished he had.

“Bollocks better get out of here,” he said into the darkness.

“Freddie,” the voice said.

"Who is that," he didn't recognize the voice at all.

"Freddie the frog," the voice said.

He hadn't been called that since school when he used to go swimming, he used the front crawl, and used his legs like a frog so the kids had laughed, and called him Freddie the frog because he looked like a big frog.

"Who the hell is that," he said sharply.

"Your wife is with us Freddie do you want to speak with her," the voice said in a mocking tone.

Freddie didn't believe in ghosts, but he was getting mighty scared.

"Look just leave me be, and leave my darling wife out of this."

"Okay Freddie we will stop messing around now."

"We," Freddie said.

"Yes, there are two of us."

"You sound both the same."

"That's because we are twins stupid," then the sound of two young girls laughing.

Freddie inched his way towards the cellar stairs he was sure they were this way. Then he banged into a wall, "Shit," he was lost in his own cellar.

Then two figures jumped onto him, and he cried out. They were small, but so strong and then one clamped her teeth into his neck. The other one hit him in the stomach, and Freddie went onto his knees. Then he felt the other one feeding from the other side of his neck, and he thought of Cromwell and this word 'vampires.'

Rosemary called down the cellar steps, "Are you okay Freddie." He was taking a while normally he would do the job in quick time, and be back.

“Service miss,” a voice called over to her and she saw that she had a customer he was not a local, and wore rags.

He smiled at her as she came over, he had short dark hair and a dirty face.

“How can I help you sir,” she put on her best smile as Freddie always said a customer was a customer no matter what they looked like.

“Can I have a pint of blood please,” the man said with a big grin on his dirty face.

“What,” Rosemary said looking perplexed.

Then a giggle from her left and another man appeared he had white hair and tatty clothes, “And a pint of blood for me as well.”

“And one for me Rosemary,” a third person this time a woman with short blonde hair.

“And two halves of blood for us Rosemary,” she looked over the bar, and saw two kids in rags. The two kids were holding hands, and they were filthy.

“What the hell is all of this tom foolery and where the hell did you all come from,” Rosemary said fear creeping into her voice. What had Cromwell said ‘vampires.’

“We’re from hell bitch,” the man with dark hair said.

Then she heard screaming, and saw the two kids and the woman attacking Tony and Colin at their table. The two kids had attached themselves to Tony, and he was not putting up much of a fight.

Colin was in the woman’s arms and it was like they were kissing, but Colin was making gurgling noises in his throat.

Rosemary backed away, “No please keep away from me.”

Her back hit the fridge behind her, and the two vampires jumped onto the bar top.

“Now its your turn bitch,” the man with white hair said, and then the both jumped on her as she screamed.

Cromwell tried to call the station, but nothing now he was getting really worried. Had all of his constables been taken was it only him now.

He cruised the streets of beach shore, and used his loud speaker to tell people to go to the church. It was the best way even if the vampires could hear it as well.

They would hear, but be on their guard for the crosses and the holy water could hurt them, yes Cromwell didn't care if the vampires heard.

"Please people if you can hear me go to the church your lives are in danger," he said into the loud speaker.

"If you can't make it to the church lock yourself inside and don't open the door for anyone even friends and family," he said saying it in a clear and loud voice.

“People are not what they seem so don’t talk to anyone, and if you can please come to the church at once.”

Cromwell sighed damn he could murder a coffee.

Hulk sat in his living room well it was his mothers living room. He hadn’t been home in years, and now he wanted more than anything in the world to tell his mother that he loved her.

But he had been around the house, and his mother was not there. He saw pictures of himself when he was a young boy. His mother still kept framed pictures of him it made his heart ache.

The reason he had moved out was his step father he couldn’t stand the man. That last day he had beaten up his step father, and called his mother a whore, and left never to have come back apart from now.

When he needed her most, she was not here for him. He had heard a few years back that his step father had passed away that had made him smile at the time. He remembered he had gone out, and got pissed that night in celebration.

“Where are you mother,” he said into the empty room, “I need to tell you I love you mother, and I am sorry.”

“I’m your mother now Jordan,” a voice came out of nowhere.

He got up from the sofa and went to the window it had sounded like it came from the fog. He could see a hazy figure in the fog.

“You’re not my mother.”

“I said I am your mother now Jordan.”

“How do you know my name no one ever calls me that apart from my mother.”

“Yes, come to me Jordan and let me hug you.”

Hulk smiled could that really be his mother, but the figure had said that she was his mother now. What did that mean.

"Come to me Jordan and I will show you what it means."

Could she read his mind!

Hulk opened the front door, and went outside into the fog.

"I'm coming mother," he walked to the figure with his arms out stretched.

He embraced the figure tightly, and then let out a mighty scream!

13

Beans and burgers was empty it had been slow since the fog started. They had a few customers the first day, but not many and today was just a wash out not one person had been in.

Sandy stood next to Lauren and said, “My god its it worth staying open.”

“I know what you mean I’m so bloody bored,” Lauren sighed.

"Maybe we should go and chat up Bernie, and get him to close the place down until the fog lifts," Sandy said with a wicked smile.

"Okay but don't you start your flirting with him he is old enough to be your dad," Lauren let out an even bigger sigh.

"As if I would," Sandy grinned.

Bernie was helping his chef Leroy in the kitchen not that there was much to do. The gridle was on, and Bernie was cutting up some Lettice and tomatoes.

"It's so damned quiet maybe I should have closed while the fog was here," Bernie said.

Leroy nodded his black head, "Yes boss I think maybe you should have."

Leroy liked that he was getting paid for nothing, but he liked Bernie, and didn't want him to waste money.

"You look so sexy today, Bernie," Sandy said coming into the kitchen with Lauren.

"What I'm wearing what I always wear," Bernie replied.

"I know that, but he just look good today," Sandy smiled at him.

"Oh, really Sandy please no more," Lauren moaned.

Bernie smiled at the two waitresses.

"What can I do for you girls then."

"Its so slow Bernie can't you just close up and let us go home," Sandy said in a sexy voice.

"I'm so bored I don't think any body is going to come out in this fog," Lauren said.

Bernie rubbed his chin and looked at the two girls, and then at Leroy, "Okay people lets close the place up and go home."

"Thank you so much," Lauren said she could get back home to her daughter now. Her mother was looking after her at the moment.

Bernie walked into the restaurant and stopped, and starred open mouthed. The whole place was full every single table was taken!

Then everyone started to chatter.

Bernie didn't notice the rags for clothes or the dirty faces.

"Oh my god," was all he said.

He hurried back into the kitchen.

"Its total mayhem out here you two go and start taking orders, Leroy start getting the food fired up."

"What do you mean," Sandy said and opened the kitchen door. The place was packed.

"Oh my god its packed," she said.

"How did that happen," Lauren put in looking into the restaurant.

"Doesn't matter how just get out there and start taking orders," Bernie almost screamed at them.

Cromwell stopped the car he could see figures in the fog was it vampires or people he couldn't tell yet. He inched closer, and stopped in his headlights stood Martin and Sally Henderson.

"Hey get in the car now," Cromwell called to them.

They got in the back of the police cruiser.

"We heard your message about the church, and were going there now," Martin said looking worried.

"Yes, what's all this about Cromwell," Sally asked him.

He smiled at them he liked the married couple they had lived in beach shore all their life's. Martin was a window cleaner, and Sally worked in the local bakery.

They were a nice couple Martin was tall and thin with short brown hair. Sally was small and plump with a kindly face.

They had been married for five years now, and still no sign of any kids. But that was there personnel business not his.

“Let’s get you to the church, and then I will explain everything,” Cromwell said.

“Look there,” Martin said pointing.

There in his head lights was a figure laying in the road. ‘I know it’s them’ Cromwell thought.

“I had better go take a look stay in the car and lock the back doors,” Cromwell said he had better take a look just in case.

He moved towards the figure it was not moving.

Laughter came out of the fog it sounded quite close. Cromwell looked into the fog it was impossible to see anything.

Then a beautiful woman appeared by his side he turned, and looked at her. She had tied back long dark hair and bright red lipstick on her pretty pale face.

"Do you want me Hudson," the woman said.

He knew she was one of them only they used his first name, and took out a bottle from his pocket.

"You are a very beautiful woman," he said unscrewing the cap.

"I knew that you wanted me, kiss me Hudson," she closed her eyes.

Cromwell threw the holy water into her face.

The creature screamed, and held her steaming face, smoke was rising into the air.

"What have you done to me," she screamed and disappeared into the fog. The figure laying in the road had also gone.

Cromwell quickly got back into the car.

"We could hear laughter in the fog," Martin said looking scared.

"Let's get the hell to the church and I will explain," Cromwell said speeding off into the fog.

Sandy went up to a table, and smiled at the family that sat around it. They wore rags and they were all dirty it was strange to her, but she wouldn't say a word they were paying customers no matter what.

"What can I get for you sir," she smiled at the man with the long looking face and bald head. He reminded her of a horse.

"I would like to fuck your arse," the man said looking at her calmy as if it was the most natural thing to say.

Sandy was shocked, and the two dirty children giggled.

"What did you say to me," Sandy asked.

Then the woman spoke she was dirty with brown curly hair, "He said he would like to fuck you up the arse."

Sandy didn't know what to do she was in shock.

Lauren smiled at the young couple sitting in one of the booths.

They were both covered in dirt, and wore rags.

“What can I get for you,” Lauren said pen poised over her pad.

“I would like a blood clot please medium rare,” the man smiled he was handsome, and young looking.

“Sorry,” Lauren said had she heard right.

Then the woman said, “And I would like a glass of iced blood.”

“Sorry, what did you say,” Lauren said looking confused.

“Oh, fuck it we would like to drain your blood from your body please,” the man said smiling at her.

One man got up, and put his hand on the kitchen door handle.

“Sandy what’s going on,” Lauren shouted as the diners got up as one.

“I don’t know but let’s get back into the kitchen,” Sandy called back. The kitchen was blocked by the large man holding the door handle he shook his head, and smiled at her.

Sandy and Lauren walked back into a corner as the crowd came on towards them. They hugged each other and cried as the crowd closed in.

Brent was home, and he threw the empty can of soup into the waste bin. He was scared oh so scared. Vampires were running amok in the fog killing people at will.

He would write about this, and he would be a best-selling author. But he needed more facts, but that was out of the question he was a writer he would make most of it up anyway.

He heard Cromwell’s message about the church maybe that wouldn’t be such a bad idea.

Brent stepped into the fog he would keep to the fences and shop fronts, and stay out of the vampire's way. He started to make his way to the church he heard laughter in the fog!

Bernie cut up cucumber, Lettice, tomatoes and onions as fast as he could. Leroy was grilling burgers and making the beans on the stove the smell of herbs and spices was almost over powering.

"The girls are taking there time out there," Bernie said cutting up an onion. His eyes were staring to water.

"You said it was full boss it will take them a while to get all of the orders in," Leroy said turning over a burger.

There was a knock on the kitchen door. The girls didn't knock they usually just walked in.

"Who is there," Bernie shouted out.

A man popped his head around the door, he had a dirty face with a bald head.

"Sorry mate you can't come into the kitchen staff only," Bernie said to the man.

"I just wanted to say that your waitresses give great head," the bald man smiled at Bernie and Leroy.

"What the hell do you mean by that," Bernie said thinking that his waitresses were blowing off the customers. They would never do that.

"I Mean this," the man stepped into the kitchen holding two heads one in each hand, he held them by the hair.

Sandy and Lauren stared wild eyed in a fixed look of utter terror. Blood dripped to the kitchen floor from the two heads, and made puddles.

"Oh my god," Bernie dropped his cutting knife, and stared in horror at the two heads!

Leroy stared open mouth his back to the grill.

Then the door opened, and in walked an army of people.

"The food is in the kitchen," shouted one man.

More people piled in and went for the two shocked men who didn't stand a chance.

Day three

14

Father Michael walked down the centre aisle the wooden pews on each side of him. He had blessed a lot of holy water, and had put it around the windows, and the door ways.

He wanted to make the church a fortress against the evil forces. He found it hard to believe in vampires it was so unreal. But Cromwell was a well-respected police officer, and would not make up such stories.

"Father Michael," the voice came from out in the fog it was loud, and he could hear it inside the church.

"Begone demons from hell," he shouted back.

"Father Michael come to us now," the voice said loudly.

"I said begone demons," he shouted back.

"Come to us we can have so much fun," this time it was a woman's voice.

"Tempters from hell," he called back.

"Come play with us father Michael," this time it was two kids voices.

"Be quiet all of you," he shouted putting his hands over his ears.

Laughter from outside in the fog.

Father Michael sat on a pew the voices had stopped. He looked at the floor, and could still hear laughter. Then there came a knock at the old wooden doors.

"I said begone demons you may not enter here," he called out loudly.

"Please Father its me Brent Odell from the local newspaper," the voice replied.

Father Michael got to his feet, and took out his cross just in case it was one of them trying to trick him.

He was up close to the door now, and put his hand on the large key.

“How do I know its you Brent,” Brent often came to mass and Father Michael knew him to talk to.

“I wrote an article on the church two years ago about the new roof,” Brent replied to the question.

Father Michael turned the key, and opened the large door. Brent came inside, and he quickly closed the door again.

“Thank god you let me in Father I could hear things in the fog,” Brent sat down on a pew, and father Michael joined him.

“You are safe now my son,” father Michael said, and patted the man’s hand.

“Thank you, Father,” Brent smiled at the priest.

Laughter from the fog louder this time, and both men looked up.

"Look what he did to my face," the woman screamed, and added, "My beautiful face."

Abraham looked at the woman with the sores all over her once pretty face.

"Isabell Your face will heal in time just keep putting fresh blood on the wounds," Abraham said.

"You can't let that Cromwell get away with this he has disfigured me," Isabell cried out loudly so everyone could hear.

They were all gathered in the big red barn again.

"He will pay don't worry Isabell," Benedict said stepping forwards, and ushering Isabell from the wooden stage and back into the crowd.

Abraham looked down at Isabell, "Why did you let this happen we are so superior to these humans."

"How did I know he had holy water he just threw it in my face," Isabell sobbed.

"Okay, okay we must all be more on our guard," Abraham heard the mumbling from the crowd.

Benedict stepped up, "Are we all putting the bodies into the swimming pool."

A hand came up near the back of the crowd.

"Yes, you there speak up," Benedict called out.

"The estate agents were all shot we didn't feed on them," a man said.

"That's as it may be but every body must go into the swimming pool," Benedict sounded cross running a hand through his bright green hair.

"No problem we will deal with that when the meeting has finished," the man called back.

"Good," now Abraham stepped up to the front, and smiled at the crowd.

"My brethren please if you wish have baths or showers to clean yourselves, and use the clothes from the dead."

Abraham had to say that, but he already knew the answer, but maybe one day they would clean themselves up.

“My name is Buck,” a man stepped forward from the crowd. He was tall and thin with long dark hair set on a handsome face. Abraham knew him he was a kind of third in command.

“We are from the grave master,” Buck said and carried on, “We come from the grave and like to be the grave.”

Abraham nodded his head they liked to wear rags and be dirty because they were from the grave. He smiled at the crowd.

“Okay my brethren it is the last day of the fog so the fog may thin in places, and let the sun through. So be very careful on this day.”

The crowd murmured its approval.

“What about Cromwell he is asking people to go to the church,” Isabell spoke up in a hard sounding voice.

Abraham nodded his head and replied, “Yes Cromwell must be taken, and we will soon go to the church and destroy the bloody thing.”

The crowd roared, and men thrust their fists into the air.

Buck looked into the swimming pool it was filling up nicely with dead human bodies.

Lance had come with Buck he was a young vampire maybe in his teens with wild blonde hair, and a rat like face.

The two men started to pour petrol onto the bodies from large metal cans. Lance went one side, and Buck the other.

They met, and put down their cans.

“You see why this was done Lance why Abraham our great leader made us do this,” Buck said smiling at the young vampire.

“Yes, so we could clean up after us, and leave no trace of what we done,” Lance smiled back.

"Oh, they will find the burnt bodies, but they will have no idea what happened it will become a great mystery to them," Buck laughed.

"Maybe they will make a movie about it one day," Lance laughed.

"Maybe Lance, just maybe," Buck patted the young vampire on the back.

15

There came a knock at the large wooden doors, and father Michael looked quickly across at them.

"Don't let them in," Brent said holding Father Michaels hand.

Father Michael looked at Brent, “I have to see who it is first my son.”

“It could be the vampires Father,” Brent said, Father Michael took away Brents hand, and stood up.

He walked slowly down the aisle, and stopped at the large doors, “Who is it,” he called out.

“Father please let us in its Graham and Heather Horne,” the voice sounded scared.

Father Michael paused.

“Please father you helped us with our mortgage when we were short of money last year, and we paid you back just last week,” the desperate voice said.

“Okay,” Father Michael opened the door and let the two in. He looked out into the thick fog and heard wild laughter and then a scream, he quickly shut the door.

Graham and Heather sat down close to Brent, “Cromwell is telling folks to come to the church so we followed his advice," Graham said, and looked at his wife heather.

"How we made it I don't know," Graham sighed.

"There was laughter and screaming coming out of the fog, and we thought we could see shapes in the fog sometimes it was awful Father," Heather said almost in tears.

"Yes, we could feel evil in the fog pure evil," Graham added.

"You are right there it is pure evil in the fog," Brent said looking up at Father Michael.

Father Michael sat down and smiled at the new comers, "While we wait for more people, I will tell you what is in the fog."

Cromwell banged on the large wooden doors. Martin and Sally at his side.

"Hurray I can see shapes in the fog," Sally said in a frightened voice.

“Yes, Cromwell please get us in quick,” Martin added.

“Father Michael its Cromwell open up man,” Cromwell called in a loud voice looking out into the fog.

The fog seemed thicker up in the hills where the church was in the streets below it was starting to thin out in places.

The door opened and Cromwell ushered Martin and Sally inside.

Cromwell smiled he saw Brent and Graham and Heather Horne. Also seated inside the church was Paul and Helen Robinson and their two kids Butch and Clayton.

Then there was Colin and Maggie a married couple and an old age pensioner Audrey.

“Well, we seem to have attracted a lot of folks,” Cromwell said he was pleased that his efforts had paid off after all, and people were coming to the church.

Markus saw the young boy pushing his skate board along the road with his foot. Markus had been in the group almost as long as Abraham, but he was still getting nowhere. How was that creep Benedict Abrahams number two it should have been Markus. Then there was that Buck getting far up the ladder as well.

That would all change one day soon Markus would take Abraham out, and become their leader he would do a much better job than Abraham that was for sure.

"Hey little boy," Markus called out.

The boy stopped skate boarding, and looking into the fog.

"I can see you who are you," the little boy called out.

The boy was right the fog was starting to thin.

"Come to me Edward, and I will show you such delights," Markus said.

“No go away and leave me alone or I will tell my dad,” the boy whined.

“I will rip your dad’s arms off first, and then maybe his legs,” Markus laughed.

Then he went for the boy, and stopped his arm was burning!

“What the fuck,” he screamed out and moved back into the thicker fog the sun had penetrated the fog and burnt his arm.

“My dad said you shouldn’t swear,” the boy called out.

Markus heard the little boy skate boarding away at speed, but he didn’t chase the boy it was becoming too dangerous now.

Anna saw the couple necking in the garden they were sitting on a wooden bench. She could hear the parents of the girl inside talking. The young girl must have sneaked out to meet her boyfriend.

Anna had also been in the group a long time, but unlike Markus she enjoyed being a follower she was not a leader. She liked Abraham, and would follow him until the end if there ever was an end.

Anna was tall and slim with long dark hair, and a rather plain looking face, and her nose was too long. But she had her fair share of boys before she was made into a vampire.

She edged closer to the young couple and saw that the fog was thinning in places this was not good at all. She stepped around the thinning fog, and got really close to the couple.

“Your hand is so cold Timmy,” the girl giggled as he tried to touch her breast inside her shirt.

“I will warm them up then Tammy,” Timmy started to blow on his fingers.

“You are so funny Timmy,” Tammy said laughing.

“Yes, he is really funny,” Anna said moving into their line of vision.

“Who the fuck are you,” Timmy said in shock.

“A peeping tom,” Tammy cried out.

“Peeping tom watching you two amateurs give me a break,” Anna laughed out loud, “But I am going to rip both of your throats open.”

“Tammy are you out there,” Tammy’s father called from the back door.

Then Anna cried out in pain as sunlight hit her out stretched hands. Flames came out of her skin, and she screamed louder and rushed back into the thicker fog.

“Dad help us,” Tammy screamed.

Her Father rushed out and grabbed the two kids, and pulled them inside. He wasn’t even angry that they had met up in secret he was glad that they were both safe. Even he knew there was evil in the fog.

The meeting had been arranged in a hurry, and Abraham was not pleased. Benedict stared at the crowd of vampires in the big red barn.

“We have to move out it is becoming too dangerous for us now Abraham,” Markus called out, and showed the crowd his burnt arm.

“The sun did this to me,” Markus said in horror looking at Abraham in the eye.

Abraham knew what Markus wanted he was a hot-headed vampire, and would never lead his group. He didn’t feel sorry for Markus, and wished the sun light had burnt his god damned head.

“Look at my hands,” Anna said crying blood tears.

Abraham felt sorry for Anna she was a devoted disciple.

“Markus and Anna, we have one more job to do before we leave tonight,” Abraham said.

The crowd of vampires looked at him.

Benedict stepped forward for his piece, “The streets are dangerous the fog is thinning badly, but up in the hills where the church is the fog is still thick.”

Abraham smiled, and took centre stage again, “Thank you Benedict yes the last job is to destroy Cromwell, and his merry band of arseholes.”

The crowd of vampires cheered, and punched the air.

“Off to the church we go my brethren.”

Isabell shouted out, “I want to feed on that bastard.”

16

Cromwell and Father Michael took a walk away from the others who were all chatting together. They walked up to the altar, and Cromwell looked at the statue of Jesus on the cross.

"I had a brilliant idea earlier I forgot to tell you," Father Michael said in almost a childish voice he seemed excited.

"Please tell me Father."

"I was putting holy water around the church, but I could only reach the stained-glass window ledge so I thought how can I put holy water all over, then it hit me like a sledge hammer."

Father Michael paused, and smiled at Cromwell.

"I love gardening you see and I have a back pack spray gun."

Cromwell smiled back, "So you used that."

"Yes, the whole inside of church has been sprayed with holy water, now let the bastards come and get us."

"Brilliant just brilliant I feel safe now father."

Abraham stopped just outside the church, and Benedict came up to him.

"What is it master," Benedict asked looking at the church.

"Do you not see it," Abraham asked.

“See what master I see a church that is waiting for us to invade it.”

“No, the whole of the inside of the church is glowing, our powers are all different I see it clearly.”

“What does it mean master,” Benedict ran a hand through his green hair he looked a bit confused.

“It means that Father Michael has put holy water all over the inside.”

Abraham turned and saw Markus, “Markus come here and join us.”

“I have a plan it may work it may not, but we will see,” Abraham said to the two vampires.

The first grave stone came through the stained-glass window. It landed on a line of pews, and smashed through the wood.

“Fucking hell,” Cromwell said, and ran for the group of people huddled together on a line of pews.

"Everyone to the back of the church now," he shouted.

The group moved to the back of the church as another head stone was thrown through a stained-glass window. This one smashed on the floor.

"We are safe inside so just stay together," Cromwell said.

"My god they used head stones," Father Michael said.

"Don't worry Father, we will replace them," Cromwell said.

"What are they out there," Audrey asked.

"Vampires they are vampires," Brent said looking scared.

"I can't believe that I'm sorry," Graham said.

"I don't care who believes it or not the fact is they are out there, and they will try and get in here one way or the other," Cromwell replied.

“Oh my god I see it now,” Colin said and went on, “The laughter in the fog the screaming they were using the fog as cover.”

“My god yes,” his wife Margaret added.

“I’m scared mummy,” Butch said clinging onto his mother Helen.

“Me too dad,” Clayton went to his father Paul.

“Be prepared for something folks,” Father Michael said looking at Cromwell.

“Cromwell nodded, “Yes they will try something that’s for sure.”

17

Abraham went to the broken stained-glass window, and looked back at his followers, "Hang back I have an idea."

Abraham made himself lift off the ground, and he floated to the broken window and looked inside the church.

"Look there," Paul said pointing to a stained-glass window.

"Its one of them," Helen said holding Butch close.

"Now you see Graham, look man," Cromwell said.

"How can he float like that," Graham said in shock.

"You believe now darling," Heather said smiling at her husband. He nodded his head.

Helen stared at the floating man with the fedora hat on his handsome head. He looked so pretty and nice, and he was smiling at her. She felt funny like she was a teenager in love again.

She put Butch on a pew, "You stay there while mummy goes," she said to Butch.

Helen started to walk towards the broken stained-glass window.

"Helen what are you doing," Paul cried out, and Cromwell turned.

Cromwell ran for Helen and he reached her not far from the window. He saw the vampire dressed in all black with a hat on his head, but he did not look into the beast's eyes.

"Helen stop," he said and grabbed her.

She started to fight him, and he grabbed her wrists then she tried to bite him.

“Helen it’s me Cromwell,” he said trying to stay away from her teeth.

“Let me go you fucker I must go to him,” she screamed.

Father Michael appeared and uncapped a bottle, and looked at the vampire and smiled at it. Then he threw the bottle at the vampire who vanished in an instant.

Helen fell into Cromwell’s arms, and sighed and fainted.

Cromwell carried her back to her family.

“You keep an eye on her Paul,” he said putting her down on a pew.

“I will,” Paul said looking at his wife.

“Mummy, mummy are you okay,” Butch cried.

Clayton just stood there looking on at the scene.

"Good work Father my god she was like a wild cat," Cromwell said to Father Michael.

"Look," Father Michael said, and Cromwell saw sun light.

"The fog is thinning out," Cromwell almost shouted out in delight.

"Markus come here now is your time to shine, and prove to me that you are a worthy vampire to stand at my side," Abraham said.

"I will do what you ask master," Markus replied.

"Be quick the sun is starting to come through the fog," Benedict said now looking worried.

"Yes, make haste Markus you know what to do," Abraham gave Markus his orders through his mind.

Cromwell patted father Michael on the back, and they both turned to walk back to the group.

The vampire came through the broken stain glass window at speed, and hit Cromwell in the back!

Cromwell went down hard, and banged his head on a pew. Father Michael screamed in pain as the vampire slashed his face with its sharp claws.

Father Michael fell holding the side of his bloody face. Cromwell also felt blood running down his face.

He got to his feet and saw the vampire sitting on a wooden beam above them. The beams had not been sprayed with holy water.

"Cromwell you are mine," the vampire laughed. Now Cromwell could see the other vampire in black at the window again looking in at the scene.

"Come and get me you fucker," Cromwell hissed he was ready to fight to the death if it came to that.

The vampire hissed at Cromwell, and then came at him again at speed. He hit Cromwell, but this time grabbed him around the waist.

“Come and met my master he has a bone to pick with you fucker,” the vampire laughed.

Cromwell was taken up, and then they started to float towards the broken window, and the waiting vampire.

Then the vampire with the hat was gone in a flash, and Cromwell smelt burning, and then he was falling to the floor.

The vampire screamed as the sun light hit him. He cursed and went out of the broken window at speed.

Cromwell hit the floor hard, and moaned out loud he heard his arm brake.

Sun light flooded into the church, and the group of people cheered. Father Michael helped Cromwell up, and he clenched his teeth his arm hurt like a bitch.

"One day Cromwell I will come back for you, and you can count on that," a voice said out loud.

"Its over Cromwell," father Michael said holding Cromwell.

"Is it over Father," Cromwell said looking at the broken stained-glass window.

Epilogue

By night fall the fog had completely gone and the line of cars and vans and coaches moved out of beach shore. The old red barn was burnt to the ground.

The windows were all blacked out and the line moved slowly as if they had all the time in the world.

“Abraham where to now,” Benedict asked they were in the lead car with Buck and Lance and Markus. Markus was burnt on the side of the face, but he wasn’t hurt too badly his clothes had caught fire saving his skin.

“That Cromwell will get it big time,” Markus cursed he was glad to be in the lead car now he was moving up the ranks at last.

“Leave Cromwell to me I will choose the day when he will meet his maker and no one else is that understood,” he glared at them all.

They all nodded their heads yes.

“Good now onwards we go to where I do not know,” Abraham said with a smile on his lips.

Cromwell looked at the burnt-out swimming pool the smell was so bad they had to wear breathing masks.

Two other law enforcement units were helping with the clean-up of beach shore.

“My god how many bodies do you think are in that swimming pool,” asked a young constable with acne and glasses on his boyish looking face.

Cromwell shrugged, “Your guess is as good as mine, but they were all good folk’s local folks,” he said tears coming down his face he had lost so many people, and a lot of them were his friends. People he had known for years. His town was in ruins.

The vampires had just left like they had never been here at all. Would they come back next year when the fog returned. He would make sure he was ready for them next time if there was a next time.

The end

www.ingramcontent.com/pod-product-compliance
Lightning Source LLC
LaVergne TN
LVHW010559160826
845677LV00013B/3186

* 9 7 9 8 8 4 6 0 7 6 3 1 0 *